The
Stormy
Night

For Arianna

I will take refuge in the shadow of thy wings
until the storms are past.
Psalm 57:1, NEB

Text copyright © 1991 by Sanna Anderson Baker
Illustrations copyright © 1991 by Fred Marvin
All rights reserved

Library of Congress Catalog Card Number 90-71488
ISBN 0-8423-6772-1
Printed in Singapore

96 95 94 93 92 91

6 5 4 3 2 1

The Stormy Night

Sanna Anderson Baker
Illustrated by Fred Marvin

Tyndale House Publishers, Inc.
Wheaton, Illinois

Outside the storm roared
and lightning leapt across the sky.

Inside
Anna lay
waiting for another flash
to illumine her room
and rattle her windows
with rumbles of thunder.

Then
from far beyond the stars
riding wings of wind
a chariot carried God
to Anna's room.
Come ride with me, God said.
His voice was mellow as a yellow moon,
and the sound of it made Anna yawn.

Before she'd finished yawning
she was sailing through a sea of stars.
Spica, Sirius, Regulus, Rigel.
God called them all by name,
and they came and danced for him.

Onward
God and Anna flew
to the edge of the Western Sea
where sharks and swordfish
whales and sailfish
finned and frolicked
and seemed to say,
> *Glory be to thee*
> *Glory be to thee*
> *Glory be to thee*
as they skimmed through the singing sea.
And Anna joined their song.

God gathered her in his arms
and held her fast as they flew.
Below them mountains danced
       hills skipped
       rivers sang
       and trees clapped their hands.
And God dropped down on their dance
a crown of flowers.

Over the meadow of morning

                 up through the sky
         up
and up
the chariot carried them
to a house made all of light.
Come in, God said.
This is my house.

Its walls were windows that touched the sun.
God went to one and said, *Anna, come.*
Countless worlds whirled below.

God spoke a word to Earth.
To the hills he said, *Be green*.
     And they were robed with grass.
To the meadows he said, *Feed sheep*.
     And they were spattered with lambs.
And everything was green and good and spring.

All about them
sparrows and swallows
swooped and soared
filling God's house with song.
And Anna sang along.
Her singing made God glad.
He gathered her in his arms
and whispered, *Under my wings,*
under my wings,
under my wings.
His voice was mellow as a yellow moon.
Safe beneath God's wings
Anna slipped to sleep.

When Anna woke
birds were singing
and sun poured in on her like honey.
She looked for God.

Then
dishes clinked
and Mother called,
"Anna. Breakfast."

The storm was past.

SANNA ANDERSON BAKER teaches children's literature at Wheaton College and writes children's books, short stories, and poetry. A graduate of the writing program at the University of Illinois at Chicago, she lives in Wheaton, Illinois, with her husband, Stephen, and their three daughters, Gabrielle, Arianna, and Anne.

FRED MARVIN, whose two great interests are children's literature and theater posters, has illustrated covers for such classics as *The Little Princess, Dune, How Big Is a Brontosaurus,* and *The Once and Future King.* He lives and works in New York City.

The Stormy Night audiocassette

Featuring a dramatic reading of the story and an original music score by Jeff Johnson, the audio version of *The Stormy Night* captures the simple beauty of Ms. Baker's words and brings Mr. Marvin's majestic illustrations to life.

Available from your local book or record store, or write to Ark Records, P.O. Box 230073, Tigard, OR 97223. Released by Ark Records; distributed by Sparrow. AKC–1273